To Dick and Joan Danckert, with my love
—R. W. D.

To Isho and Naomi
—Y

Joy & Happiness Yoshi 11/17 '96

SIMON & SCHUSTER BOOKS FOR YOUNG READERS

An imprint of Simon & Schuster Children's Publishing Division

1230 Avenue of the Americas, New York, New York 10020

Text copyright © 1996 by Ruth Wells

Illustrations copyright © 1996 by Yoshi

SIMON & SCHUSTER BOOKS FOR YOUNG READERS is a trademark of Simon & Schuster.

Book design by Paul Zakris

The text for this book is set in 14-point Flareserif.

The illustrations are rendered in color dyes on silk.

Manufactured in the United States of America.

First Edition

10 9 8 7 6 5 4 3 2 1

Wells, Ruth.

The farmer and the poor god : a folktale from Japan / retold by Ruth Wells; illustrated by Yoshi.

p. cm.

Summary: A poor god living in the attic of an unsuccessful family prepares to move with them and causes a reversal of their fortunes.

ISBN 0-689-80214-5

[1. Folklore—Japan.] I. Yoshi, ill. II. Title.

PZ8.W485ar 1996

398.2'0952'02—dc20   [E] 95-12338

THE FARMER
AND THE
POOR GOD
A FOLKTALE FROM JAPAN

Retold by
RUTH WELLS

Illustrated by
YOSHI

SIMON & SCHUSTER
BOOKS FOR
YOUNG READERS

Many years ago, high in the mountains of Japan, there lived a poor farmer and his family. It seemed to the farmer that the harder he worked, the poorer he got. This wasn't true as he was a dreamer and didn't work very hard at all.

It also seemed to him that the poorer he got, the more children he had. This wasn't true either. There were only four children. But the farmer and his wife were so unhappy that the children ran here and there all day, fighting and shouting. It just sounded like there were a lot more of them.

One night the farmer whined to his wife, "We are so poor, we must have a Poor God."

Now about that, the farmer was absolutely right. In the attic space of their small hut, there lived a Poor God.

As Poor Gods go, he was a kindly sort. He liked the farmer and his wife and he liked to sit in the dusty, cobwebby attic, listening to the children play. But he was a Poor God, and a Poor God is something to be avoided. A Poor God, BIMBOGAMI, is bad luck, and everybody knows that once Bimbogami gets hold of you, you will never be truly rich.

The wife said, "I think you're right. Maybe if we move, life will be better. We could go in the middle of the night, while the Poor God is sleeping. He won't know that we have left and we'll be free of him and his bad luck."

The farmer hugged his wife and danced around the hut. Finally he knew why he was poor, and it wasn't his fault. "That's a good idea," he said. "We'll leave early in the morning, before the sun comes over the mountain."

They packed their few belongings in a knapsack, unrolled their FUTON, and tried to sleep. The farmer began to imagine the life they would have once they were free of the Poor God. Maybe he would work as a SHOKAN, an overseer on a large estate, and he would tell other farmers what to do. Or maybe he would become a SAMURAI, a brave and loyal warrior who would guard the lands and the family of a nobleman. The farmer began to get so excited about his new life that he couldn't sleep.

He got up quietly so as not to wake his wife and went outside. There, in the moonlight, he saw a stranger weaving sandals.

"Who are you? What are you doing here?" the farmer demanded.

"I am the Poor God who lives in your attic. I heard your plans for going to another village so I am weaving sandals for the journey."

The farmer stamped his feet, first one and then the other. Then he wailed—so loudly that he woke his wife.

"Wife, Wife. Here is our Poor God. He knows we are leaving. He is planning to follow us. We will never get away from him and his bad luck!"

The wife tried to console him, but it was no use. He moaned and groaned all night.

In the morning the Poor God waited, still weaving sandals. He had made six pairs for the journey, because straw sandals wear out quickly. And even though there wasn't going to be a journey, the Poor God continued to make his sandals. He thought it was a good thing to do, to take a small pile of straw and weave it into something practical like a sandal.

From time to time that day the children stopped playing to watch the Poor God's long thin fingers work the straw. While they watched him, they were quiet and he made each child a pair of sandals.

That whole day and night the Poor God sat beside the house weaving his sandals. The next morning there were twelve more pairs. He tied them in a bundle and hung them from the roof of the hut.

The next day he found some straw that was a deep red and when he wove that with the yellow straw from the farmer's rice paddies, his sandals were beautiful.

And so it went for some time.

The farmer and his wife sulked.

The children shouted and fought with one another.

And the Poor God made sandals.

The Poor God accumulated quite a store of sandals. They were sturdy sandals, woven with straw from the stalks of rice that the farmer grew. The Poor God found that he could dye straw a deep blue and he created patterns of yellow, red, and blue as he wove.

One day a man from the village came down the road and saw the Poor God at work. "Old Man, those are beautiful sandals you are weaving."

"Thank you," said the Poor God, who had never heard such kind words. "I have so many. Please have a pair. And take this pair home to your wife."

The villager thanked the Poor God and took the sandals home.

The next week another villager passed the hut.

"Old Man, I heard of your sandals from my neighbor. He said they are sturdy, but also very beautiful."

"Thank you, sir," said the Poor God. "Take these pairs home to your wife and children."

The farmer's wife happened to hear this conversation and she repeated it to her husband. He stopped sulking long enough to say to the Poor God, "Don't give those sandals away. Say they cost a bag of rice."

The Poor God agreed that was a good idea and the next day, when two villagers came by, each took a pair of sandals and left a bag of rice.

The third day another villager bought a pair. Instead of a bag of rice, he left a chicken. The farmer watched all this from inside the hut and thought, Maybe if I took those sandals to the village I could sell many pairs.

The next morning the wife bundled up the sandals and the farmer slung the pack over his back. When he returned that night, he was carrying six chickens for roasting, a new cook pot for his wife, and a piece of candy for each of the children. Not a single sandal was left.

"Poor God, you must make more sandals for us," the farmer said.

"I will," said the Poor God, "but I need you to bring me more straw from your rice paddies."

The farmer and his family did what the Poor God asked. Soon they were all busy harvesting straw, dyeing it different colors, helping the Poor God make sandals, and carrying them into the village to sell.

They were all so busy they hardly noticed how their lives were changing.

There was plenty of food now and nobody was hungry.

The children played their games out in the fields while they worked with their parents. They ran around, shouting and laughing. And nobody thought they were loud at all.

The wife, who had worried so much, sang as she worked, and once she even laughed out loud.

The farmer learned how to make sandals. And wonder of the centuries, this man who had been so lazy as a farmer was really an artist. He made sandals so beautiful you would rather hang them on your wall than wear them on your feet!

But for the Poor God, the changes were strange.

Usually a Poor God is scrawny because he is hungry and raggedy because he is poor and nobody likes him because . . . because . . . why, because he's a Poor God!

But this Poor God was getting a little chubby around the middle. His ragged clothes were mended and his dusty attic clean. And strangest of all, the family began to love him. The Poor God knew it was time to move on and make room for FUKUNOKAMI, the god of good fortune, so his family could be truly rich.

SHOGATSU, the new year, is the most important holiday of the whole year in Japan. And this year, in the days leading up to SHOGATSU, the family cleaned the little hut and then cleaned it again. They cooked a special meal of rice cakes and rice wine to welcome the coming new year. This year the farmer was sure they would be truly rich.

It is the custom as midnight approaches for the priest in the temple to ring a massive brass bell. He rings it slowly, 108 times, and as the tolling bell echoes across the valley, each family opens their door to welcome the new year.

But in the farmer's house, just as the bells began to ring, the Poor God appeared, ready to say good-bye.

The wife, who now sang all the time, wept. And the children, who now rarely fought with one another and were obedient almost all the time, clung to his legs. "Why are you leaving?" they wailed. "We love you."

"I must leave. If I don't, you will never be truly rich. See, here is the Rich God, come to take my place."

And sure enough, standing at the open door was the Rich God with his fat, smiling face and jeweled kimono. He pulled at the Poor God's arm.

"Hurry," he ordered. "You must be gone before the new year is here. This is my family now and I am here to make them truly rich."

The Rich God pulled the Poor God one way and the children pulled the Poor God another. Somebody threw a pot of water and there was so much hollering and commotion that the farmer had to shout to be heard.

"Stop," cried the farmer, who was now an artist.

Everybody stopped and all you could hear were the bells and the farmer's voice, firm and strong.

He said, "I thought I wanted to be truly rich. But there is singing in my house and laughter. I create beauty every day of my life. We are already truly rich."

And with that little speech, the family pushed the Rich God out and slammed the door behind him just as the bells ended. They hugged their Poor God and sat down to their meal to celebrate their good fortune.

Over the years the farmer and his family made many pairs of sandals. Each pair was different and each more beautiful than the one before it. The children grew up and married. They built houses close by and their children played in the yard outside. And on the eve of each new year, the farmer gathered his family about him and told the story of the sandals and the Poor God who lived in their attic.

"It's a good thing for that Poor God," he would say. "Who knows what might have happened to us if not for him!"

The Poor God had always been very quiet and after a while the family hardly ever heard him. He had also been very shy, and after a while the family hardly ever saw him. It's not that he went somewhere else, it's just that after a while he wasn't there. Like the song of a rare bird; for the briefest moment you hear it and then it's gone. You listen hard, but you never hear it again and you wonder if it was ever there at all or if it was something you just imagined.